T0128916

It Is This I Am

The Inner Mentor

MARSHALL D. GRAYSON

BALBOA.
PRESS
A DIVISION OF HAY HOUSE

Balboa Press books may be ordered through
booksellers or by contacting:

Balboa Press
A Division of Hay House
1663 Liberty Drive
Bloomington, IN 47403
www.balboapress.com
1 (877) 407-4847

Because of the dynamic nature of the Internet, any web
addresses or links contained in this book may have changed
since publication and may no longer be valid. The views
expressed in this work are solely those of the author and do
not necessarily reflect the views of the publisher, and the
publisher hereby disclaims any responsibility for them.

The author of this book does not dispense medical advice or prescribe
the use of any technique as a form of treatment for physical, emotional,
or medical problems without the advice of a physician, either directly
or indirectly. The intent of the author is only to offer information
of a general nature to help you in your quest for emotional and
spiritual well-being. In the event you use any of the information in
this book for yourself, which is your constitutional right, the author
and the publisher assume no responsibility for your actions.

Any people depicted in stock imagery provided by Thinkstock are
models, and such images are being used for illustrative purposes only.
Certain stock imagery © Thinkstock.

Print information available on the last page.

ISBN: 978-1-5043-7752-2 (sc)
ISBN: 978-1-5043-7753-9 (e)

Library of Congress Control Number: 2017904756

Balboa Press rev. date: 03/30/2017

Contents

Preface

I witnessed two life-ending incidents less than a month apart. A nineteen-month-old baby girl and a sixty-six-year-old grandmother died from misdirected violence. The baby girl died while her father used her as a shield in a gunfight with police. A teenager shot the grandmother with a stray bullet that missed his intended target, a rival gang member, and hit her at the bus stop. Bullets meant for someone else struck them and ended their extremely valuable lives. That is justification enough for any work that anyone does to combat ignorance and violence.

There is a solution to the hunger, ignorance, and violence that permeate our environment, so it must be said. This solution demands redirection in every aspect of our lives. We must see with the eyes of inner vision. We must concentrate our mental energies on researching how things are connected, combined, interrelated, and intertwined, instead of how to divide things up!

We use the principles of division as a means of ascertaining knowledge without realizing that employing that principle in one aspect of life, without conditions, leads us to employ it in other aspects of life. One example: After discovering the atom, we discovered by splitting atoms, we could release tremendous amounts of power, which we placed in a bomb that killed ninety thousand people in Japan within forty-five minutes of hitting the ground. This can also be seen in how we use something as simple as skin pigmentation to divide families, societies, states, and nations. Most of our wars have been about seeing "them" as different from "us" so we have the right to wipe them out and take their resources. Have we not let the division principle get out of hand?

When we direct our keen, investigative minds to see how creating is about putting things together, instead of breaking them down, we will start seeing evidence of harmonious unity. Harmonious unity permeates the universe. It is more the rule than the exception. The atomic soup that makes up our skin is about the harmonious dance of protons, neutrons, and electrons, whirling about each other at tremendous speeds, creating miniature galaxies that bond with each other to create something tremendous: you and me. This is much like the stars orbited by planets, whirling about each other at tremendous speeds, creating solar systems that bond together to make up macro-galaxies, which bond together to create universes.

So, we start with ourselves. Let us perceive, if only for a moment, the incredible interplay that takes place as we read this writing and consider what it says, feeling a mix of emotions coursing through us as these clips of reality resonate with something deep within. Realize that as you interact with these thoughts, they bond with all the other thoughts that make up your stream of consciousness, creating new thought streams and new expressions of actions and reactions, shaping the mechanism that is your experience in life. How wonderful this interaction is. How wonderful we are. It is extremely fascinating, just as fascinating as how the thought to pick up a pen generates the electrical impulse that signals our skeletal and muscular framework to extend our fingers, bend them, and grasp and lift that pen to share this moment in ink. All the while, cells die and are born in the skeletal and muscular framework that engages in picking up that pen. It is so simple and so marvelous. How wonderful!

Take a moment to visualize any animation of a tuning fork you've ever seen. As it is struck, vibrations emanate upward and outward into the universe. Visualize, if you will, instead of the tuning fork, your body actually sitting there, not necessarily being struck but vibrating nonetheless. And the different vibrations coming off your body are different levels of consciousness.

For example, your physical being has a level of consciousness that interacts with your conscious awareness, often in the form of the intelligence that keeps your lungs inhaling and exhaling, your blood flowing, and your heart beating, all without you thinking about it. Oftentimes, this intelligence tells your legs to move when you have the urge to dance, the fingers which key to hit next at the piano, your attention which direction to focus on as you read, and so on. You have a mental level of consciousness that is extremely busy right now, following this train of thought, pulling the meaning out of words being shared, and so on. There is a level of consciousness that is your emotional mind. It maintains a functional equilibrium to the inner maelstrom of emotions constantly coursing through you. Your emotional mind is a very vibrant level of consciousness. Then there are the myriad of transitional consciousnesses as your awareness sorts through the constant flow of thoughts, feelings, sensations, and states of being. All these processes go on all the time.

On the outer fringes of this striation of consciousness is this level of consciousness that is united with all consciousnesses in all other phenomena. It is deeply entrenched in it all yet untouched by it all. It is referred to religiously by many names and as many concepts. It has been referred to as buddhahood, the Christ Mind, atman, and the godhead and, from the semisecular realm, the superconsciousness and the collective unconscious.

Take a moment to imagine this, your highest level of consciousness taking form, to visit and converse with your ordinary state of consciousness in some not-so-ordinary ways. Journey with me for an infinite moment into that interaction, for It Is This I Am.

It Is This I Am.

Chapter 1

The First Talk

I sit here, nearly prone, on the beige couch. My eyes are shut enough to block light but not enough to entice and embrace sleep. One quick opening flutter, and I glimpse the soft bluish glow of the TV, its usual blaring attack of my senses a mere droning irritation.

"Is it bedtime yet?" I ask. And there it is, in my own voice: "No." My voice is answering my question. But it is more resonant, deeper, and smoother than I have ever heard my voice be. My awareness is such that I can trace a verbalization from the utterance to the thought just before. But I can't this time, not with this no, because it is so singular, without physical, psychological, or emotional trails to trace. It is just that curiously perplexing no. *I must be really tired*, I think.

"No, we are not tired; we are ready." The response comes with the same calm, measured, untraceable singularity. I instinctively close my eyes. I see a lively, cosmic scene, much like the photos NASA shoots from satellites, with stars, planets, comets, satellites, and meteors. But this scene shows a two-story shadow of a hooded head and shoulders. I look at the back of a huge human figure, and it turns toward me. The hood keeps the facial features shadowed. Only the tip of the nose is bathed in light. The eyes open, and in those eyes, I see the same cosmic scene with stars, planets, comets, satellites, and meteors. In those eyes, I detect a smile of comfortable knowing. The lips move, and I hear, "No, not tired—ready!"

I am startled and sit straight up, my knees barely missing the beveled edge of my round glass tabletop in front of my couch. "What the—?" I shake my head and then palm my temples and shake my head again. I am way too old for fanciful hallucinations, visions, lucid dreams, or whatever.

"Open your eyes," the voice says.

I look out into my living room. There are the off-white, textured plaster walls. There is the bluish glow of the TV and the bouncing text screensaver on the computer monitor against the northern wall. There is the black loveseat with its contrasting cream pillows adjacent to my glass coffee table. My black bass guitar sits serenely in the corner. Everything is in its comfortable, familiar, safe place.

"Ready."

Once again, my eyes close. When I open them, my vantage point is from within the hood's shadow. My vision is expansive; no, actually, it is infinite. There, before me, dance galaxies with white-hot centers and spiraling arms containing millions of stars. I feel my body shake. I'm passing out.

I awaken with an urge to go to the bathroom. Standing there in the dark, I follow the trail of the physical urge pressing into my haze of sleep, stirring me to rise and head to the toilet. As I stand here with my eyes closed, partially as a remnant from my sleep, the cosmic scene continues. "Wow, is this a memory or a dream?" I ask aloud to no one in particular.

"Neither," that same deep, resonant, smooth voice responds again. "It is now. It is true vision. What we see is who we are as eternity; how lovely."

I stumble back toward the couch but then decide to head for the bed instead. I can trace the trails of that decision. However, the communication at the toilet was a singularity. I've gone down the rabbit hole. This must be the experience that has led many lucky ones to psych wards and not-so-lucky ones to cardboard condos under bridges and freeway overpasses. I hear the question or conclusion, "Is this craz—" form and decide against asking it. I do not need another deep, resonant response.

"We'll sleep now."

Yeah, right. I want to know what the...You know, sleep wouldn't be so bad right about now, I think. I'll let the small electric fan on the dresser blow the hot air around, put on some nature sounds, and drift off. Oh yeah, I have to get to work in a few hours.

Chapter 2

Joining

The alarm is set for 4:20 a.m. As always, my feet hit the floor between 3:54 and 4:02. I turn on the soft light on the nightstand, stretch, and consider whether I should reset the alarm and lie back down. Deliberations can be such fun, especially ones with myself. Closing my eyes usually adds a bit more drama to the negotiations. Instead of the blackness of my eyelids, I see the night sky and this two-story-tall translucent figure walking in that sky, headed for earth—hood and all.

Damn, damn, damn, it's starting again. Well, I'll be ready this time, I tell myself. The figure's strides cover city blocks, and as he moves, I feel the air collecting in the hollow of the hood. I hear the blare of the traffic between his strides. I smell the magnolia blossoms and jasmine shrubs along the street. And then he is upon me. I am bathed in a warm, comforting glow emanating from us both. The glow intensifies, and I feel this melding take place as he, with tremendous ease, contracts his huge, translucent body into mine, like a genie getting sucked back into a lamp.

"Ah, there we are. This is such a joy." That deep, resonant, smooth voice, now emanating from within me, has the added dimension of soothing calmness. I remember

4

anxiousness coursing through me at first sight. I have to remember, because I have no anxiety now.

"Why do you keep saying *we*?" I ask. "Are you some sort of composite, or is my suspicion correct that you're referring to *you and me*?" I feel the smile on our faces.

"It is simple. *I* can be written big or small; it is the same *I*. I will leave the *we* now that I and I have been introduced and consciously joined, having attained at-one-ment. I have always been, and forever shall be, embracing and intimately immersed in every particle of the space-time continuum. The fabric of your being is this I. No more will I know distinction, separation, or division; the creator, creating, and creation are one. Look at the farthest star, the tallest mountain, the twinkle in a baby's eye, and a mirror, and see the creator. It Is This I Am. Now, know thyself."

I am not ready. I am joyfully teary-eyed, wonderstruck, and speechless. As I perch on the edge of my bed at 4:20 a.m., the alarm goes off, and smooth jazz fills the room. I sit there in a state that looks and feels a lot like bliss. The air and all it touches have a bit of luminosity in them. Everything glows. Peace permeates the air. As I begin to stir, every action is a sigh. A soft, soothing hum fills my body; it is life in harmony. My choice is simple: I must either embrace this or confront this, but it will not be denied. As in all situations, my reaction will dictate my experience, which my choice guides. Heaven's or hell's gates open through choice.

"Catch up. You chose quite some time ago. I am here!" the voice says.

Now, thoughts that for years seemed fragmented and unrelated fly through my head at the speed of light and expose their interconnectedness and wholeness. Visions, memories, and dreams all mesh together, revealing a common thread. I have been headed here all my life.

I'm gonna be late. Damn. How do you punch the clock from this far out of the box? I wonder. *There are 1.6 million kids who need a quality check done on their teachers.*

Chapter 3

The Heart

"The infinite, creative essence of the universe is not limited to your definition, until you know. Before asking how all this came to be, follow cause-and-effect." Riding in the fast lane down Route 105 is not the place for this dialogue or monologue (whichever), especially if it's accompanied by those grandiose visions. Just two minutes to the end of the freeway, and not a word. So, maybe this time, only that message is needed.

One more block, and I'm in for the evening. What is happening in my chest? I say to myself. I feel a faint warmth in my heart region. Parking in my spot and ready, I feel that warmth again, but not so faint—more radiant now. The intensity makes me close my eyes. When I open my eyes, I see the skin of my chest dissolve. It loses its color and texture and exposes my ribs and heart as if acid had splashed directly onto that area. In the very center of the heart, I see pulsing light and the infinite It Is This I Am sitting in lotus position. He raises his head and opens his eyes.

He says, "The heart is the seat of the mind. All essence is the mind, from which all phenomena issue, and within, the mind has being. Being is eternal cognition: the living-knowing essence. Joy is the highest and most natural life condition. It Is This I Am. No time to question sanity; this revelation is earned. Ponder it deeply, and enjoy."

I exit the car, and my steps are similar to those of someone who is drunk; I am unsure and staggering. I feel the asphalt under the leather bottoms of my boots, but my head seems detached. Stumbling all the way, I make it to my bed.

Chapter 4

Joy and Remembering

Morning comes in too harshly, especially since I am still dressed in yesterday's clothes. The blinds on the bedroom window break up the eastern sunlight streaming through. It never fails, though: one beam of light finds my eyes and pierces my eyelids. So I awake squinting. A few inches from my nose, glowing and floating in midair, about the size of an apple, is the now-familiar It Is This I Am. He opens his eyes.

"Before moving, remember" is all he says. My eyes shut as if following an unspoken command, and the memory starts.

I had pulled the duty of being a security guard for a friend's Christmas tree lot several years before. One night, I sat in my van, parked in a lighted, two-block-long shopping-center parking lot next to the fenced-in trees. I had an extension cord drawing power from the lot's lighting system for the portable heater in the back of the van. I decided to use the solitude to fill my mind with the teachings of *The Kybalion*, Ram Dass, Maharishi Mahesh Yogi, and several other sources in my pursuit of spiritual evolution. All of a sudden, I had an epiphany: the creative energy of the universe awaits a consciousness willing to ask for what it wants.

Without a moment of doubt, I formed the request: "To the Mother, Father, and Son of creation and being, please show me a sign—a sign that goes just beyond my ability to explain with the knowledge base I have." Having voiced the request, I then surrounded that thought with a golden bubble and released it into the night sky. Never giving it a second thought, I returned to my studies.

On the pages of the book I read, the ink seemed to animate and lift off the page. I closed my eyes, rubbed them, refreshed my coffee, and went back to where I left off. The ink lifted again, this time faster and with more animation, looking like the waves you would see on a hot day traveling down a long stretch of road. It moved from the page to fill up the van and then went out the window to above the trees in the lot and onward to the horizon. I was dumbfounded to the point of speechlessness. I watched this unfold until the waves touched my eye and then all disappeared. I racked my brain and could not, with all I had come to know, theorize or explain what was happening. I believed I was seeing the answer to a prayer. I couldn't wait to express the experience to my lover at home and relive it.

Just as I got to the part where the waves touched my eye, I remembered the heater in the back of the van. I realized how, with the window down and cold air pouring into the van, I could just be seeing convection waves of hot air mixing with cold, producing the illusion of them filling the van and the night sky. As I tried to explain it away, the waves appeared and instantly filled the bedroom, spilled out the window, and filled the early-morning sky.

My lover exclaimed, "They do look like heat waves! Wow, this is fascinating." I sat in awed suspension. The waves refilled the room, floated across the bed, reached up to touch my eye, and disappeared. My prayer's answer was witnessed and confirmed.

As if a director in a studio has ordered, "Fade to camera 2," another memory starts. The coastal scene has me sitting on a jagged rock ledge jutting just over the ocean crashing underneath. The waves are strong and high enough to throw a salty mist on my face. When one is truly receptive, tender is the kiss of nature. I sit cross-legged with my arms meeting in my lap, poised in calmness. A single tear, an expression of the joy I feel, rolls down my cheek as an eternal moment of meditation subsides.

The sound of a lone seagull's cry breaks the silence and draws my attention to its flight. There, on the end of his tail feather, are those same dark ripples that were in the air. The very same waves that were above the Christmas trees and filled the bedroom on that night in December are now here in broad mid-May daylight. As the gull flies across my field of vision, those ripples stretch to reach the edge of the horizon, fill the sky, touch my eye, and disappear. Another tear streams down my cheek, and the joy I thought had dissipated rises up within me tenfold. I suddenly know what holy ground feels like.

Before the tear can reach my jawline and fall to the ground, I hear the voice of It Is This I Am. "Ah...the sweetness of being awakened aliveness can be very intense, intoxicating, and seductive. It is so often missed when attention is outward-bound, hunting, gathering, fearing, and fighting. Just be and experience the wholeness of being. Just beyond time, space, and personality is being. And being is holy and sacred. It is the very essence of your nature."

Simultaneously, we speak, "It Is This I Am," and we smile, and we join. I choose through an inaudible declaration: *If this is crazy, then crazy I'll be, but I will do nothing to impede this happening.*

Several weeks later, I realize my days seem so drastically different. As a stalwart creature of habit, I have not altered my activities. I'm doing the same things, but I'm getting different results. A certain air of detachment and a greater depth yet a lighter attitude enhance my interactions and relationships with people, places, and things. I notice much more seamless movement throughout my day. I sense wholeness in my ponderings about my day. I feel calmness throughout my day.

"All of life waits for the return embrace," It Is This I Am says. "All of life caresses you during every moment, but fear blurs the viewing of that caress. Insecurity murmurs the sigh of that caress. Doubt numbs the skin to the touch of that caress. But, oh feel the bliss of sharing an embrace with the all."

"Where are you? I don't get to see you this time? What's up with that?" I ask.

"On an overcast day, does the sun cease to exist?" he responds. "Faith based on what is seen is easy; faith based on knowing creates joy."

Chapter 5

A Gorilla in the Mist

Another lazy afternoon, and I can definitely use it. I have no chores or visitations planned. I have just a treasured, uncluttered day. I want to take a nap. So stretching out with my feet up and a pillow behind my head seems the appropriate position. As I close my eyes, I begin to relive a long-ago trip to the zoo. I am in the great-apes area. Actually, I am on the landing of a set of stairs that lead down to a walkway just in front of the great-apes area. I stand behind and above a crowd gathered in front of the gorilla enclosure.

The enclosure resembles the base of a mountain, with huge boulders, tropical bush, a fallen tree, and a little cement pond. Just to the side of the pond sits the crowd-pleaser—a huge silverback male gorilla. He is intoxicating. Every feature, every muscle is chiseled. He entertains the crowd and feeds himself with the greatest of ease. He pauses and looks above and beyond the crowd as though searching for something he senses. His eyes meet mine, and the searching stops. I see a spark of light in his eyes, and then his gaze returns to the crowd. He resumes his show of begging with one hand, catching and eating with the other. When someone in the crowd throws a peanut beyond arm's length, he notes it, but it goes unfetched. He seems to know another is on its way but closer. The hand that motions for more is always going, even while stretching to catch. This is pure poetry in action.

Then he stops, looks in my eyes again, looks at the pond of water, and looks back in my eyes. His actions scream, "Pay attention!" He resumes his begging and catching. Ever so slightly, I see his buttocks shift to the side, lifting slightly on one side. Then his lower back muscles contract on one side and relax on the other. The muscles continue shifting up his back over a period of two to three minutes, giving him an off-center and slightly backward tilt. It looks as if only his will keeps him upright. He relaxes and lets gravity push him over.

As he seems to fall over, he extends an arm to brace himself on his palm, swings his head around, grabs a drink of water, and returns to the sitting position to beg and catch. He uses one continuous flow of motion from unbalanced sitting, falling over, and quenching his thirst to returning to a balanced upright position, begging, and catching. My jaw drops as I realize not only did this ape demonstrate the conscious use of gravity to accomplish a task, but he expended the least amount of energy to get the job done. As I stand there evaluating whether I need a reality check, he once again peers above and beyond the crowd to look me in the eye. He returns to his begging and catching, and in reverence, I bow. Such a beautiful lesson in releasing others from preconceived identities and efficiency of energy—such a wonderful memory. I feel blessed.

In the center of the enclosure, a mist begins to form and expand until the entire enclosure seems engulfed in the mist. This is not part of the original experience. In the mist, the head of It Is This I Am emerges. "I am in all." He pauses; I ponder. "The self is all-pervading, permeating all times, all spaces, all things, all places, and all beings. It is being. It is without bounds, yet it binds all. It is without form yet fills all forms; It Is This I Am. The self is the conscious fabric of eternal creating; It Is This I Am. Just beyond your space-and time-confined personality, just beyond the illusion of separation, It Is This I Am. Know this self; experience bliss."

The mist, the enclosure, and the gorilla fade to black, and I sleep.

Chapter 6

Fantasy

"Some sort of fantasy. You think this is some sort of fantasy. After all, you have seen, remembered, and experienced. All of this is just a product of your imagination." It's as though I've walked in on an argument already in progress. In the parking lot of my apartment building, It Is This I Am stands just in front of me, towering about nine feet tall, with an intensity in his look that would bend steel.

He says, "In the sky above, find a cloud. Really see that cloud, close your eyes, and picture that same cloud over the Big Island of Hawaii. See that cloud just over the top of the mountains of Hawaii. Open your eyes. Where is your cloud? Know the limitlessness of being."

I feel a separation, and it saddens me. In the midst of my sadness, I feel as though I am rising off the ground. Lo and behold, I am off the ground and slowly being placed in the chest of It Is This I Am. The definitive lines between my skin and his fade until there is no distinction.

He says, "Know thyself, know life, love thyself, and love life. At the juncture where the infinite, creative mind meets the finite, individualized mind, one becomes the other. It Is This I Am. A conscious union produces joy. Sit in this awareness for a moment, and create a wave of peace. Now, project that wave of peace out to embrace all you see, touch, smell, hear, and taste! With eyes shut, visualize the earth you sit within, surrounded by a vibrant, pulsating heart. With every beat of this very alive heart, the amount of love and peace throughout the entire planet increases. This is a powerful meditation, and in the mind of the all, it is the reality of the moment!"

Chapter 7

Bubbles of Light

I seriously enjoy sitting still on a washcloth in the middle of the tub while the steamy, hot shower pours all over me. It kind of takes the chill off the porcelain. It is one of those nurturing things I do for me that I've really come to appreciate. It is an environment conducive to reflection.

I just let the hot steam turn the concerns of the day off and the inner visions on. I usually start with deep breathing as a means of calming the body. I just close my eyes and really feel the experience. I let each thought that crops up continue through my mind without stopping it to attach conscious attention, the energy magnet, to it, until those countless thoughts turn into so much mental white noise. Releasing my awareness from slavery to my thoughts, slavery to my physical vehicle, and slavery to my emotions is such a freeing experience. Here in the steamy water, peace permeates the air.

Now, to watch the water running down my face, I open my eyes. A little translucent blue bubble of light about the size of a dime flies through the air. Quickly, a white one, then a pink, a yellow, and a purple one follow it. Their flight brings them into alignment one atop another right in front of my face, where they just hover and glow. This sight fascinates me. In unison, their glow intensifies, making a clearing in the steam around them. In that clearing, they draw atoms out of the very air and form the outline of a body in a seated position. It Is This I Am speaks.

"There is a level of your being that is very subtle. It is pure awareness. The more you consciously dwell in this awareness, the more it becomes the dominant state of being. The more you allow it become the dominant state of being, the healthier the body, the calmer the heart, and the more expansive the mind become. It is very subtle but extremely powerful. It is without boundaries, without distinctions, just beyond the limitations of time, space, and personality. It is the essence of all phenomena. It Is This I Am."

A wellspring of appreciation flows through me. Over time, I have really come to embrace these interactions. I straighten my posture out of reverence for this encounter. In this moment, I touch a place of deep love. It is not a love of something or someone; it is unfathomable, undeniable, and unconditional love. It fills the entire room. I feel joy.

"This is your nature, your real essence. This is your real identity. It Is This I Am. This level of your being is eternal. At this level of being, all essence is united. What you call *your being* is actually *all being*; It is life. It Is This I Am. Before that which you discern as space came to be, It Is This I Am. Before that which you regard as the beginning of time began, It Is This I Am. Drop the ego and its need to own, manipulate, and control all it sees. It is not adequately equipped. Expand your heart enough to bathe all life in love, and joy will be your result."

The body of It Is This I Am fades into the bubbles of light. The bubbles of light lose their alignment atop one another and fade as they fly off into the steam. I melt into the steam-nurturing experience.

Chapter 8

The Audition

The forty-foot palms seem to dance together as they sway in response to brisk winds outside. From the Laundryland Wash and Dry window, I have a great view of the scene outside of swaying palms, bustling traffic, and rain-laden clouds heading in from the north. It sparks a memory.

The clouds appear heavy with rain as I travel down the familiar 105 Freeway toward work. Needing a distraction from the snail's-pace traffic, quite unusually, I turn on the radio. A commercial blares out through the speakers to those who believe they have a message to share with the world. A new reality show, *Preaching Masters*, is holding auditions that afternoon, from 3:00 p.m. to 6:30 p.m. I don't know what makes me take down the number, call, and point my car in that direction after work; it just feels right. When I hit a wall of traffic on the N-405 Freeway, I question why am I going. What do I think I have to say?

The atmosphere at the audition site is a potpourri of excitement, tension, nervousness, and anxious anticipation. The buzz is electric. I watch as preachers, ministers, and motivational speakers parade about. Some talk about their congregation, their church, and their clientele. I feel a certain affinity for a few of them; they aren't affiliated with or representing any organization. This is a competition, and folks are sizing each other up. Some seem to be rehearsing, referencing note cards, Bible verses, and typed and handwritten speeches. I decide to put my attention elsewhere.

I decide to focus on the site. I take in the lay of the land. Just beyond the overcrowded parking lot, I see a row of wonderful flowering bushes. I put my attention there. Among those bushes stands a four-foot metal artist's rendition of a garden scene complete with a bench and two children playing. As I seek to squeeze out every nook and cranny of beauty the artist wanted to convey in the sculpture, I hear my number called. I thank the artist for the respite.

Through this maze of a building filled with cavernous rooms I find people with headsets and walkie-talkies flitting in and out. They look extremely focused and busy. I am ushered into another waiting area in a dark corner of the building. At least it has a couch. I sit and wait. Finally, after an eternal twenty minutes, I am led into one of the many cavernous rooms. It is a filming and recording studio filled with lights, cameras, microphones, sound-recording equipment, and the technicians who go with all that stuff.

I stand face-to-face with one of about fifteen filming crews and a panel of judges. They lay out the procedure for me, tell me to relax, and give me a cue to speak. I have no prepared speech, no notes, and, until this moment, no idea what will pour out of my mouth—not a clue. I take a deep breath, and it flows.

"I don't have a clue what my message is! I do know that on the atomic level of things, there is no definitive line between my skin and the air surrounding it. And it's the same air surrounding all of you. On the atomic level of life, there are no definitive lines, no divisions, no separations between any of the phenomena of life. On the most basic level, life is all intermingled, intertwined, and connected, including all of us in this room. Any belief based on separation is therefore an illusion.

"Looking at life from this perspective, I can see the divine unity in life. I get a new definition to that possessive term *my life*. My life then becomes all I see, hear, feel, smell, and touch. There is nothing outside this term, *my life*. It is all-inclusive, from the most distant star on the edge of the known universe to the nearest grain of sand on the closest beach. Each and every thing and everybody is included in *my life*, including that part of my life I call *me*, *myself*, and *I*.

"There is another aspect of this perspective, this point of view. That aspect is what occurs in one's intuitive cognition. It is apparent that there is a very subtle level of one's being; that is pure awareness. The more one consciously dwells in this awareness, the more it becomes the dominant state of being. The more it is allowed to be the dominant state of being, the healthier the body, the calmer the heart, and the more expansive the mind become. It is very subtle yet extremely powerful. It is without boundaries, without distinctions—just beyond the limitations of time, space, and personality. It is the essence, and it is within and makes up all phenomena.

"This is one's nature, one's real essence, one's real identity—yours, mine, and everyone else's. It Is This I Am. This level of one's being is eternal. At this level of being, all essence is united. That which is called *one's being* is actually *all being*. It is life. It Is This I Am. Before that which you discern as space came to be, It Is This I Am. Before that which you regard as the beginning of time, It Is This I Am. Drop the ego and its need to own, manipulate, and control all it sees. It is inadequately equipped. Expand your heart enough to bathe all life in love, and joy will be the result.

"The self is all-pervading, permeating all times, all spaces, all things, all places, and all beings. It is being. It is without bounds, yet it binds all; It Is This I Am. The self is the conscious fabric of eternal creating; It Is This I Am. Just beyond one's space-and time-confined personality—just beyond the illusion of separation—It Is This I Am. Know this self, and experience bliss.

"To taste true bliss, combine this perspective with the ultimate creative force—love—and tap tremendous power. All one needs to do is love one's life and, in so doing, love all life. See the implications. Feel the effect. Infuse it with wonder. Heal the planet."

I become silent as I realize what I am saying is very real to me. My presentation has passion, conviction, confidence, and peace. The silence is not only mine. Except for the almost-inaudible hum of the lights, I hear nothing. The panel sits with pencils and faces frozen.

"Thank you. I really don't know what to think." As if coming out of a haze, the director pauses and then continues. "You'll receive a call from us soon. Thank you."

When the call comes, it tells me I would need to go live in the project house for at least three months for the show's filming. It then dawns on me that it is a reality show with a focus on entertainment. The essence of my beliefs would just act as fodder for the drama of competition. It is a living arrangement I have to turn down.

Chapter 9

Infinite Living Mind

Sitting quietly in my apartment without obligations or distractions has become an enjoyable experience. In the last two weeks, I've had this pleasure happen maybe eight or nine times. I wonder about my It Is This I Am experiences.

I sense a shadow come over my head as though I just pulled on the hood of a robe or sweatshirt. I see the glass tabletop in front of the couch. I lean over to peer at my reflection, and though quite unexpected, it is spectacular. The hood surrounds the outline of my face; however, my eyes are portals into deep space. I hear the word *wow* exploding from my mouth.

"We see all from this perspective—from the vision of the infinite living mind," It Is This I Am says. "Listening is easy. Believing is a bit more difficult. Accepting is harder still, but applying—that's where the work begins. Please understand all phenomena are manifestations of the living mind. It Is This I Am. All grasses, all grains, all beings, all planets, all stars, all galaxies, all universes— all are thoughts manifested in the living mind. The living mind is all-inclusive, all-pervading, all-permeating; we have heard this before. Repetition allows hearing to become listening. Listening allows for consideration.

Consideration with an analytical filter allows for believing. Believing is an essential step to accepting. Acceptance allows for expansion. Expansion allows for a clear vision of the self, which rests in the physical, spiritual body as bliss. Bliss is a very valuable state of being.

"Rest in the vision of the living mind, and breathe in and out the state of bliss. Keep the vision always present, and remember our life force follows our attention. Perceive the formula. Realize the cause made with each breath. Manifest each action, each thought, each reaction, each nonaction from this divine state of being, and bathe the world in peace. Staying blissful attentively will project your life force out as love. It is only natural. It Is This I Am."

Chapter 10

Teatime

Inam Bakery and Restaurant is one of those rare places that seems to nourish the spirit as well as the body. Sitting in one of the box-window seats presents prime viewing of the sidewalk through one of those pristine and precious historic districts every city has. One of the busiest four-lane streets in this city, one of the country's largest cities, passes right in front of Inam.

Across the street, leaning against a white-barked shade tree, smiling brilliantly, It Is This I Am stands. With a nod, he moves directly into traffic without so much as a glance toward any of the cars, trucks, or buses bearing down on him. As I watch him pass right through two tons or more of the metal, plastic, glass, and rubber of cars, trucks, and buses over and over again, it only surprises me how easily I accept these supernatural activities. Then he moves straight through the glass, wood, and brick of the box window to place himself right across the table from me. Not usually one caught speechless, and catching a glimpse of the approaching waiter, I tense in anticipation of responding.

"Welcome to Inam. Would either of you like to start with coffee, tea, or water, or are you two ready to order?" the waiter asks us. With a very kind wave of a hand, It

Is This I Am allows the waiter to understand we aren't ready. "I'll give you time to review the menu," the waiter says. And he is off to another table.

"He sees you. You're interacting with him, but how?" I ask It Is This I Am. "Help me wrap my head around what is happening. I...I ..." I pause, drilling down to deep, deep stupor, wide open to explanation.

With the calmness of a deep ocean and a smile that only breaks on the right corner of his mouth, It Is This I Am whispers, "Reality never has been, nor will it ever be, restricted to any definition. All the laws of the sciences—all the precepts, concepts, theories, et cetera—are still in their infancy, still evolving...It Is This I Am still becoming. It Is This I Am. Who can apply finite rules to an infinite being? Release us from the prison of a restricted perspective. As we expand our perspective of what is, more of what is can reveal itself to us; more expression of It Is This I Am moves through us. This is a lovely class we've chosen for today."

"Are you guys twins?" the waiter asks us, returning with a steaming pot of chai tea and two cups. I do not remember ordering this. "I mean, it's uncanny how much you look like each other. It's like I'm looking at one being in two bodies. It's just uncanny."

We sit, sip, and observe the rise of joy within that accompanies knowingness. As joy increases, so does the glow of spiritual energy around all living things. Ascension affects all.

Chapter 11

Himalayas Float

"But what am I to do with this gift you've brought? How do I ..." I start to say, but I trail off. The question seems so imperative that I nearly miss this query's environment. Sitting on a cloud about five hundred feet above the Himalayas, legs crossed and facing each other, It Is This I Am and I float effortlessly.

"It is no gift," he responds. "It is the result of a choice made long ago. It is like the one little hair popping out of your chest at thirteen. When the time is right, that which is needed for ascension appears. You are already doing what you need to. Pay attention to your interactions with others on a daily basis, and hear how your life impacts theirs. Listen to the respect, compassion, and sincerity you share with others and they with you. You have begun to change your respect for life and living beings. Seeing all living beings as emanations of the one self, you now move with fierce compassion.

"Realize, as you do, that which resides in you resides in all who share this existence. You share who you are with all others through your thoughts, words, and actions. Your thoughts, words, and actions are the outward manifestations of how you perceive your being. Keep your attention on the thoughts flowing through your mind. Watch which thoughts you give your conscious attention to and which you let flow unimpeded. Your conscious attention is the subtlest of energies. It is thought food. Watching your thoughts provides you with the opportunity to select which thoughts receive the energy of your attention. This process transforms your thinking. As you transform your thinking, you transform your world."

Chapter 12

Astral Journey

The early-morning hours are so quiet. From 2:00 to 4:00 a.m. is an especially quiet time. This is one of those especially quiet 2:00 a.m. mornings. I must have dozed off at about 8:30 or so the previous night. So I lie here at 2:30 a.m., rested and alert. I am too far from rising time and too sleep satisfied to doze again. This is a great time to do some directed relaxation.

I begin with conscious, deep breathing, paying attention to the in breath, the out breath, and the gap between the two. This acts as preparation for consciously relaxing each of my extremities. I start at the feet. I stretch the toes and visualize the accumulated stress lodged in my body as dark green liquid flowing out of my toes' pores and dissipating once it hits the air. Then the toes go limp but feel completely energized. I move from the toes upward through the feet, calves, knees, thighs, groin, lower back, and abdomen, causing each muscle group to release those stress toxins and feel light and invigorated.

My energy level rises. My visualizations become more focused. I continue my directed relaxation technique toward my heart region. All of a sudden, I feel and see a luminosity emanating throughout my body and seemingly lifting out of my body. It is like my essence is rising. My senses move with this rising luminosity. It looks and feels like a complete separation except for a silver cord attached at the belly button. I recognize that the luminosity forms an exact duplicate of my physical body.

My sense of who I am floats just above my body. I sense all is well with my physical body. I know all that is taking place is for the best. I sink into the feeling of peaceful floating until I can view my entire room from the ceiling. I push upward a little bit and move through the attic and rooftop. I see the top of my building and the tops of the trees and nearby streetlights. I exert another push upward, and I see the lights of the city stretching for miles in every direction. Farther up still, I see the ocean lapping the beach to my right and the barely snow-capped mountains to my left.

I look above to see where I'm headed, and I notice just before the canopy of stars appears a very thin layer of luminous dust that seems to undulate and flow. I fly into it. As I enter this layer, I realize it is enormous in its depth and breadth. It is filled with that luminous dust. I am drawn to what looks like a center of concentrated light. There, sitting cross-legged, back as straight as a board, with one arm resting in his lap and the other arm stirring a pond of liquid light with a stick, It Is This I Am quietly beams.

He says, "Here is the peak of being. It is the thought stream of creation. It is the backdrop of darkness that is the void of thoughtlessness or pre-thought— emptiness, as it has been called. It Is This I Am. In a fifty-foot wave are millions of drops of water released from the curl. Since they see themselves as single drops for a moment, they feel separate and fear their own mortality. Then they fall and comingle with the body of the wave, the rest of the ocean, the rest of themselves, and they realize their fear was based on the illusion of separation. All phenomena issue from the thought stream and think themselves separate, but just as the water droplet returns to the water that is the ocean and awakens to its greater self, so too do all phenomena awaken to the truth of their essence at the appropriate time. It is this that our journey is about.

"The power of choice dictates which thoughts, in the myriad of thoughts you think each day, will carry your focused, intensified conscious attention and magnetize all associated thoughts in and around this thought stream to themselves. The sharpness of your focus and depth of your belief in your intensified conscious attention, or faith, will determine the appropriate time for that belief to manifest. Faith is the connection point, the funnel into and out of the thought stream of creation. Great faith creates a strong and intense connection. Please, now understand the intricate relationship between consciousness and power. It is the desire to become an asset in the evolution of mankind, as man awakens to the responsibility of being co-creator of his universe, that creates this journey. This journey is endless, for it is life, and It Is This I Am!"

It Is This I Am then grabs the lapels of the robe he wears and spreads them and his chest to reveal a golden, pulsing heart. It pulses a beam of intensely bright white light that hits me in the middle of my forehead and propels me back to my bed. I feel whole, energized, and more alive than I have ever felt before, and I realize It Is This I Am.

Chapter 13

Assimilation

I see flowers in all their vibrant color, stretching toward the sun, spraying beauty in every direction, kissing and caressing any and all in their field of perception. So it is with the grass, the trees, and the birds and their song. Each time I pay strict attention and give heartfelt reverence to every rose, tree, and blade of grass that comes into sight, in that moment, I am blessed with a precious relationship with nature! It's as though these creatures bringing me such blessings consciously share in that preciousness.

My hearing transforms through acceptance, as I now feel each sound resonate down to the cellular level, and those sweet, harmonious vibrations add vibrancy to my whole being. Feelings rise within from a very deep place of calmness as a result of choice rather than as a reaction to the environment, and therefore, the feelings are more harmonious than discordant. Those times when the discordant ones filter in from the environment, I know to allow them to pass through unimpeded. These things and more happen on a daily basis. I hear my conversations with others with a new ear and speak my responses from deep within my life. Each moment has an awesome quality when I give that moment my conscious attention.

The path I usually take to the grocery store has its fair share of flowers, which is a boom to me. When I get to the corner, there is a well-worn footpath that goes through the flowers just off the sidewalk leading to the bank's parking lot, which sits in the southeast corner of the lot. About halfway up the slope of the path stands a young oak tree. I see two young girls, probably seven and six years of age, stop at the tree and spy me coming their way. I am three steps into the slope and a total stranger to them. They stand frozen by the tree. I can taste their confusion and anxiety. I hear them discussing turning around, but it is too late; I am right upon them. They won't look me in the eye.

"Does either of you know me?" I say. Without waiting for a response, I continue. "Have we ever talked? Have I ever spoken a mean word to you? Have I ever done anything to harm either of you?" With social norms set aside, I dive directly into the heart of the matter. I only pause long enough for the wheels of thought to start turning. "Look in the tree above us at the birds sitting on the limbs, and listen to the sound of their song. If I am truly someone to fear, don't you think they would know and fly off?" I look at them softly and pass just to their left to move on up the path. I feel a nervous energy in me and wonder what effect that conversation will produce.

When I turn my head in their direction, the youngest smiles and waves good-bye. I feel victorious joy well up inside me. She will never see the tear of joy her wave creates.

Just a step away from the bordering curb of the lot, my sure-footed steps slip. I instinctively reach for the ground and the curb at the same time. Before I can reach either, I feel a tug on my overcoat and look up to see It Is This I Am dressed exactly as I am, holding me by the arm and pulling me up off the blacktop.

"What was that about?" he queries in a quite matter-of-fact way.

"What? You mean the conversation back there? I could not stand the unearned fear that filled the air between us. You heard that? Where were you?" I did not see him until the very moment I reached for the earth.

"Who did you think was singing in the tree?" he says.

Chapter 14

Comfortable Deviancy

I stop every now and then to look at my reflection in store windows. I recognize the face under the closely trimmed beard and the mustache that covers the top lip. I identify the big western-style suede hat with the brim broken down all the way around, sporting a peacock feather stuck in the band around the crown. The black calf-length naval officer's double-breasted overcoat with the shiny gold buttons and wide lapels was not designed to always have the sleeves rolled up to the elbows, but that is how I keep them. The *I Luv U* pin sits right over the heart. I complete the outfit with a pair of dress boots and a case carrying my bass guitar.

I don't often think about how this vision appears to others, but I do notice that I get a wide berth wherever I travel. The vision I project seems to match the difference I feel inside. I am aware that I do not exactly follow a particular trend, dress to impress, or fit in with any group. I have a bit of a deviant projection, but it feels so natural, so right. When the isolation of this look becomes a bit much, I seek out a quiet space where I can pull out my bass, plug in my portable amp and accompanying headphones, and thump my heart out. I keep pen and paper handy just in case one of these bass lines creates a melody and a song wants to use me as an opening into this realm. Being more of a lyricist than a musician, I really thrive on the energy of creating, or rather capturing, thoughts whose time has come for expression. I sense the essence of It Is This I Am in every line I write.

I walk along the familiar path in between buildings through this industrial complex I sometimes visit. I begin to feel the warm tingle I associate with the creative flow. Maybe it's time for a bit of lyrical whimsy. I notice out of the corner of my eye the most striking purple-and-black winged butterfly. It lies on the leaf of an evergreen bush, and for just a moment, our eyes meet. The moment intensifies, and the flap of his wings seems to last for minutes, not milliseconds. I am speechless and motionless, but I have an appointment that spurs me to move.

Before departing, I bow, and I catch his eye again. As I move, so does he. I notice his flight takes him to another evergreen bush about fifty feet ahead. He sits and waits. I come upon this bush in fascination that I would have an opportunity for another close-up encounter with the same butterfly. This is phenomenal. I approach in calmness, and our eyes meet again. I move again in the direction of my appointment. He flies up about fifty feet and waits on another evergreen bush. We're in a traveling relationship. I meet his eyes once more. The two folks at the bus stop watch this activity with a kind of wonder on their faces.

I tell my purple-and-black winged friend how thankful I am for the company on this journey. He flaps his wings in that extremely slow fashion. I appreciate the acknowledgment, and as he takes wing this time, I know he will fly directly over the building I'm about to enter, so I wait and wave as he disappears just beyond the edge of the roof. I catch the eyes of the two at the bus stop, and there is this moment of knowing we have shared a wonderfully rare and unique moment in life.

I recognize this experience is meant to provide all involved with the absolute proof that all consciousness is one consciousness and that one consciousness is the wisdom that manifests as life.

Chapter 15

Lunch with a Squirrel

Standing in the rear of the crowd, I realize my initial reaction to the request to attend this rally was on point. The dean of student affairs had strongly suggested the students of San Diego City College needed to be represented at this rally, so I needed to attend.

The rally focuses on money, unions, and politics. This event's organizers represent a level of decision making that does not need nor have any interest in the input of the president of the associated student body. However, I find myself in beautiful Balboa Park, really attempting to make sense of it all. I double-check the agenda, and in between speakers, I slowly and respectfully vacate the premises. I don't leave the park entirely, just the noise and clutter of the rally.

I walk along a sidewalk that runs parallel to a shallow canyon running the length of the park and nearly hidden by a row of chest-high bushes. As it's late fall, the bushes are mostly barren of leaves. I notice a tree limb that looks nearly as thick as the trunk, only a foot or so above the ground. It is unusual to see such a huge limb that close to the ground. I venture through the sparse bush and discover I am only seeing the top third of this tree. It's actually rooted at the base of the canyon. I sit on the limb and let my feet dangle just above the ground. On the back swing, my feet dangle above the canyon.

I get that rare, fleeting glimpse of aliveness in the tree and bushes. More than an enhancement of depth of color and texture, this glimpse lets me perceive the tree's life force. I can only perceive this when I am quiet in mind, calm in body, and emotionally still. I follow each breath in and out, and the perception intensifies. Now, the area all around me has this aliveness popping out at me from every direction. My calm, quiet, and still state intensifies as well, and I want to project this perception through the bushes onto the sidewalk. And so I project the vibrant, peaceful aliveness right to the far edge of the sidewalk and a square yard in both directions. Within this corridor of peace, there is no controversy, no conflict, no tension, nothing inharmonious. I experience the bliss of union with all things alive, and it is powerful.

A dog approaches on the far side of the bushes. He walks into that section of the sidewalk, and all his hairs bristle to attention. He uses his nose and eyes to survey the area, and he traces the intensity to where I sit. He walks away slowly, softly, and at ease. Three men jogging on that same sidewalk, discussing an upcoming merger with a corporate rival, step into that section of sidewalk, and the conversation stops. Once they step outside that corridor, they stop and question each other about the pause. Having no explanation, they reach back to resume their conversation. The two incidents intensify the bliss I'm experiencing.

In a hollow in the trunk where the limb I'm on joins the tree, a squirrel pops his head out, sniffs the air, grabs an acorn from within, slips down the limb to sit next to me, and nibbles on his nut. For what seems like endless moments, the squirrel, plants, and I sit serenely in this blissful unity. I open my mouth and ask the squirrel if he is enjoying his lunch. With those words, I identify him as being separate from me, the limb, the nut, and the grass, and in that moment, the unity fades. The bliss diminishes, and the squirrel looks at me with disappointment. And now with distrust, he gathers what is left of his nut and runs off to his hollow.

I learn that in the state of conscious being, any thought of separation has the potential to interrupt bliss. I am thankful for the moments of being conscious of the unity that flows through all life and for the bliss that permeates that state. I am thankful for the contact with It Is This I Am for leading me here.

Chapter 16

Use

When my vision is really on, I can see the energy streams among living things touching each other. I can see the welcoming warmth of acceptance of the flowers as they receive the beauty of birds' song. It is the dance of lovemaking in its finest form. The vision of the interconnectedness of living beings gives me peace and joy that know no bounds. I know bliss! When my vision is on, It Is This I Am floats on a cloud right around my heart region. I no longer need to have the vision to know it is happening. My joy, my bliss deepens and expands with each breath.

I now know why in the throes of creating, we have no need for food, rest, or any other creature comforts. The joy of creating nurtures the body with the energy emanating from the essence of life, expressing itself through the creative activity. The essence of life uses the brain's content and says this shall be the expression, and while it takes form, the form expressing it gets replenished, refreshed, fueled, and pleased. Every result of creative expression manifests the essence of life. This must be the reason why the universe continues to create forms through which to express as it creates itself out of itself. There is sacredness in the divinity that is creativity.

"The universe is beyond reason and understanding. Understand it is its own reason. Approach it in acceptance, and its lesson is simple; it is life that is sacred. Each breath is sacred. All that is sacred is precious, and what is precious is easy to overlook, especially when perception focuses only on finding a reason or a practical use for what it perceives. Perception without the purpose of finding reason or practicality, without the need to analyze or categorize for understanding, is awareness. Awareness without a utilitarian focus is meditation and a tool for expansion. As one seeks how to be of use instead of how to use, one seeks the natural flow of phenomena. One's vision expands, and so does one's definition." So comes the message from just around my heart region, and the cloud that was just around my heart region is now under my feet as I get lifted about six inches off the ground. It Is This I Am!

Chapter 17

A Nut of Wisdom

A break in the day's usual activities gives me time and room for a meditation session, creating a pathway to that aspect of being just beyond the physical space, just outside time and deeper than personality. I transport myself to that tree on the edge of the canyon in Balboa Park and experience the same quiet of mind and the bliss of union. In the hollow of the tree appears a squirrel. He joins me on the limb with a nut in his grasp. Then without provocation, the squirrel looks at me with disappointment and now with distrust gathers his nut and runs off to his hollow. He then pokes his head out of the hollow, looks deep into my eyes, and returns. With nut in hand, he sits next to me, and the distinction dissolves; the bliss of union remains. At his side sits It Is This I Am.

He says, "In the experience of unity, the oneness that defies explanation, the joy of being, is all there is. The creative essence of life is that joy, is that unified field. It is consciousness in its most potent state. It has shed the illusory limitations of its form; be it flower, boulder, ant, or elephant, it is being. It Is This I Am."

I hear the cracking of the nut paradoxically in the distance, and within. The squirrel proceeds with lunch as though he sits alone on the limb. His calm, serene demeanor permeates the entire scene, including that which I identify as my body.

"As identification with the body dissolves, as distinctions of separation diminish, being beyond form emerges. It Is This I Am! Being is without restrictions; it inhabits all forms, as the innermost occupant of all phenomena. Consciously assimilating the knowingness of being leads to awakening. Awakening to the true essence produces pure joy."

I can feel my jaw muscles work in unison with the squirrel chewing on the nut. As we swallow the meat of the nut, it produces an energy surge that starts at my core and emanates through every extremity, heading up through my skin. As light shines through each and every pore, all I perceive begins to radiate and glow. It is the rising of joy.

"Acceptance of this process is the grace of love. Being in the grace of love is creation. Creation is continuous. That which is outside time has no beginning or ending. Being in the grace of love is eternal."

I can sense the glow of light from my pores blending with the glow from the limb, the squirrel, the grass, the sidewalk, and the bushes. Everything in sight glows, and all glows blend. The glow around It Is This I Am radiates in an intense pulse with a distinctive hum. As it pulses, his body expands to take in the entire scene. Everything gets captured by his expanding form, from the edge of the park to the edge of the horizon, on into deep space.

"Not tired, ready." He pauses. "Ready to receive, and ready to give!"

Printed in the United States
By Bookmasters